The Goddess Who Earned Her Stripes

Vaishnavi S Kabadi

Ukiyoto Publishing

All global publishing rights are held by

Ukiyoto Publishing

Published in 2023

Content Copyright © Vaishnavi S Kabadi

ISBN 9789360164553

All rights reserved.
No part of this publication may be reproduced, transmitted, or stored in a retrieval system, in any form by any means, electronic, mechanical, photocopying, recording or otherwise, without the prior permission of the publisher.

The moral rights of the authors have been asserted.

This is a work of fiction. Names, characters, businesses, places, events, locales, and incidents are either the products of the author's imagination or used in a fictitious manner. Any resemblance to actual persons, living or dead, or actual events is purely coincidental.

This book is sold subject to the condition that it shall not by way of trade or otherwise, be lent, resold, hired out or otherwise circulated, without the publisher's prior consent, in any form of binding or cover other than that in which it is published.

To Maa and my dearest sister Vaijayanthi

Contents

A "No" Caused Havoc	1
Soapstone	4
Kali	6
A Bitter Discourse	8
A Bloodied Shore	10
The Weapon I Possess	12
Withering Away	13
Red	14
Safe	15
Miracle	18
Panchaali's Endurance	19
To Learn Late	21
Ego And Agony	23
Brittle	24
The Goddess Who Earned Her Stripes	26
Can I Breathe Again?	27
Dust	28
Dear Daughters	29
Plates And Glasses	30

The Affliction Man Gives	32
Unclean	33
Brand Me with Your Version of Womanhood	34
Tinted Windows	36
Roots	37
If Men Wrote Sensuality Sensibly	38
Radhe's Raas	40
Dear Maa	41
Chasing Rainbows	43
Women And Climaxes	44
Women of the Home	45
To My Love	47
Bloom	48
I've Learnt Over the Years	49
About the Author	*51*

A "No" Caused Havoc

In our "mother" land
Blood has run dry
On women's thighs
And shame
Bottled and sold in frenzied numbers
Like they sell alcohol in dim lit villages.

The vulva, opened
Like the seals on envelopes
And breasts groped in bustling buses
Blood flowing through bruised lips
And cigarette butts branding skins.

Shame swells
Shame reeks
In families when women come home bleeding.
Shame swells
Shame reeks

2 | The Goddess Who Earned Her Stripes

Not on rapists or abusers
Shame swells
Shame reeks
On victims of crimes
Like guilt branded
And ignominy in infinity
Their attires held liable
And six pm curfews accountable.

The women in our "mother land"
Whose throats have run dry
Their voices suppressed
By laws and their families
Inside these dingy walls
Of shame and humiliation.

A "No" caused havoc,
So he ripped open these clothes,
Thrust rods, fondled breasts and burnt bodies.
Rage! Seething! Like rivers in outrage
And lust,

Killing the dreams of her being.

Candle marches and protests later,
Our laws
Banned tinted windows on cars and buses
Launched helpline numbers and other promises.
Justice is served through half baked laws
Justice is served through unfriendly grievance cells
Justice is anything but hanging the rapists.

Soapstone

They carve me on soapstone,
Place me on a pedestal,
Smear vermilion on my forehead
And seek forgiveness for their sins.

In their homes
When they return inebriated,
They forget prayers and remember rampage.
No more remorse, only maim.
I collect their sins
While they offer me flowers
To return favors I cannot bequest.

They return home, sullen and snarling,
At those women who nurture their children.

They bathe me in milk and almonds,
Fearing my wrath; they bow down to pray,

And beg me to erase their sins.

They treat me like purity
While my kind that resides in their homes
Sleep in tattered mattresses
Stained with their menstrual blood.

My kind are born
With the heart of a thousand mothers;
Fire and blood of warriors and wreck;
Wisdom and knowledge of goddess Saraswati;
And the wrath and calm of river Ganga.

You cripple the courageous,
Dilute their depth,
Condense the capability of my kind;
And then immodestly bow down
To seek forgiveness for your sins?

Kali

A garland of skulls around her neck.
Her tongue as red and rouge as blood.
It's true what folklore says,
She drinks up all dreadful desires
And buries lecherous men
Under the blood-red river bed.

Her skin, a midnight blue, the womb of resistance;
And her eyes, wrathful, feared in all of existence.

Goddess Kali sticks her tongue out,
Widens her eyes
And stands naked in gait alongside her mighty blade,
With a prowess that pushes people to beg.

But centuries later, her kind lie in their deathbeds
Their skulls crushed and tongues cut off;
Their eyes, cold and dead.

They fear sticking their tongue out
And standing tall with gait;

They beg for forgiveness
To escape
From the wrath of ash and death.

A Bitter Discourse

When I was young and innocent,
I believed intelligent conversations brewed among men at parties!
The patterns of bitter smoke and spirits
Would brew a heaven of ideas, I'd often assume!
The ideas certified by the high masculine discourse, I'd call it.

As the clock ticked from seven to eleven
Conversations would turn to lewd laughter;
Sane men to scurrilous, swaying dancers;
Politics to bitter scandals.

While they would converse drunk, litter floors and laugh lewdly,
The women would scrub kitchens, burn fingers and feed children!

Corrupt to the core; vile as villains;
Oppression in their bones; repression in their tones;

Conversations covetous; laughter lecherous.
I'd learned that men at parties
Often brewed hell
With their filthy and foul demeanor.

A Bloodied Shore

They wanted a bloodied shore
After vows and thrusts.

Oozing
Wounded
Pure
And ripe enough to give birth.

The room didn't smell like love;
The roses on the bed
Rotten and forlorn;
A white cloth to prove her chaste;
And some gaudy plastic to ignite the fire
While consent,
Like spilt milk
Lay astray

You'll hum your way to sleep
The way your mothers and sisters did.

But today
You've made your family proud
Even if it means
You've offered a man
Your blood!

The Weapon I Possess

I've had my breasts groped
Not by lovers
But by strangers on the bus;
Penises flashed
By men I've never known;
And been heckled
By loathsome, lecherous men I've never met.
And yet they've taught me
"Silence is a potent weapon".

Withering Away

In our motherland
Women have the habit of withering away.
Like the leaves in autumn
And metal when it rusts.
Neem, the only view from their kitchen window
While they stir red concoctions in brass vessels.

Mothers and daughters,
From daybreak till nightfall
They wither away
From black to gray tresses.

In homes where love should reside
Resides the residues of their being
And silence.

Red

My body is an object
For you see fit to exploit it for pleasure
But you want to test it for red
After taking your wedding vows.

My body is a playground
For you to play till sated and bated
But finally abandoned
For not offering you red.

In between white silk sheets
You want to explore an object
And play moans and murmurs
Till the last of your heart's content.

But you dare not touch this object
If it has been touched by the hands of another,

So you leave HER
In shambles and abandon.

Safe

The Goddess Who Earned Her Stripes

In my distinct inventory of moments
I find my mind goes back
To those summer afternoons
That felt like indie music.
My mother's cotton saree,
The smell of cloves and garlic
The cream curtains of our room.

A garden of love,
A nest of affection and a song of comfort
That we'd often record on our cassette tapes
Embraces that cured, stories of palacial glee
And tangled arms weaved happiness
Like the yellow champa flowers that bloomed in our garden.

The distant sounds of trains,
Dust unsettled,

Shining in the beams that cut through the cream curtains.

The fragrance of comfort and calming contrasts.

Encompassed in slow time, breathing free,

Mother's touch brought me serenity.

Encompassed in an alchemy of love

My childhood home

Was safe and soothing.

Miracle

Vermilion on foreheads,
Rings on their toes,
Bangles they adorn
And cycles that flow.
And as if the glory,
The cycles
And hands that work with vegetables weren't enough.
Women make miracles
With pots and pans
And homes and children;
With plants and poetry
And make-up and men;
With books and bodies
And calm and courage.
You truly are a miracle.

Panchaali's Endurance

When they returned to Hastinapur
After bloodied battles and bloodstained wounds;
Did Panchaali tremble
While walking through the intricate staircases?
The ones she had been dragged through
Her wounds still of fresh blood
And her hair that had come undone
Like a fierce river!
Did Panchaali burn the single saree?
The one that brought catastrophe during the events at the Dyud Sabha.
The one that women draped during their monthly cycle.

Did Panchaali grieve her children's death?
The ones that had given her joys of motherhood.
The ones that were a part of her heartbeat.

Did Panchaali grow careless?

While braiding and draping her tresses and sarees
The ones that Dushassan brutally laid his hands on?

Did Panchaali's endurance lead her to fragility?

Did she drape her sarees and braid her tresses in sheer carelessness.
A few strands pouring out,
The pallu uneven
And kohl missing from her once fierce eyes!
Did Hastinapur feel like home to Panchaali?
While the lewd laughter and language of 100 brothers echoed inside its walls?

The strength of Yajnaseni
And all women
Is often dilapidated inside the walls of their own homes!
Through wonder and wreck,
And worry and woe
They try to build homes out of misery.

To Learn Late

My mother sees beauty in unchaste things
And photographs them on her mobile phone,
The angles aren't perfect, the clarity blurry
But in all the imperfection,
This I do know
I've learnt to appreciate little things because of my mother
And know that she appreciates beauty
In nooks and corners.

My aunt painted for the first time,
A little imperfect, a little out of line
And grammed it for her 50 followers.
"Is it good enough?", she had asked me uncertainly
But in all the shadow of doubt
I know that she found her medium of expression
In colours rare.

My grandmother clad herself in a Kurta for the first time,

A little shy, a little reluctant.

"Do I look good?", she asked me?

She looked beautiful in an unconventional way.

But in all the reluctance

She told me she had felt liberated to wear a Kurta

After years of cladding herself in the seven yards.

Ego And Agony

They love us
They love us in their raging agony.
When the tip of their cigarettes burn our skin;
When the words that wound leave their mouth;
When their rage boils down to scars on our bodies.
We obey, like dutiful wives,
To be hurt, burnt and maimed.
By ego and agony.
We shiver and call it love.

Brittle

The women with voices
Often forget those women
Who do not have voices!
Women confined in drab brothels;
Women in "safe place" orphanages
Or women adorning purple damages;
And the little women,
Sold like chinaware,
For labour, sex, salaries and seduction.
They wither away, rusty,
Without love, empathy or voices.

Our empowerment is fragile,
Pieces of weak glass and egos.
Our empowerment is self-serving,
Self-sufficient and self-satisfactory.
And our empowerment is sitting in warm corners,

Relishing in lavish gossip while shaming women.

The empowerment we have is brittle, messy and partial,

Rusting away without equality.

The empowerment we have

Isn't empowering anymore.

The Goddess Who Earned Her Stripes

There are glimmering white threads
Hooked and engraved on my being
And yet my body isn't ruined.
In fact, this is where a woman grew.
My hips, my breasts and my inner thighs
Gleam like slithering rivers
With a beauty so potent
My smooth skin splits like glass.
A gleaming arrow in the flesh
A queer, quaint and luscious flaw.

I trace my skin through rivers and glass.
I'm the goddess who earned her stripes.

Can I Breathe Again?

I'm a dry leaf

Fallen off a tree

Under pressure I tear apart

And your expectations disintegrate me.

When you step on me hoping it would bring out my best,

I tear apart little by little.

The pieces of me float, lifeless like nothingness;

Hoping I'd have the chance to breathe again.

Dust

The air here vanquishes me;
I've become a mere memory on a photograph;
A raindrop that evaporates;
A dead leaf fallen.
Famished, forgotten and far away.

Maybe I'd reside in bitter corners of hearts;
But dry up like a well when the pain subsides.
Maybe I'd become a memoir
Put into words, by people, for a day or two.
Maybe I'd just be a photograph
Seeking justice during candle marches.
Or maybe I'd just be a speck of dust
Disappearing into thin air.

Dear Daughters

In our homes
To love is a crime.
And our honour,
More vital than happiness.
To love is a sin
But with permission, a win.

Daughters,
They rely on you for honour.
And place your deeds in brittle glass vases.
You break one and oh what a shame!
The bitter wrath and shame your folks have to face.
You can rust away in unhappiness
You can disintegrate to ash
But bring not your parents, shame.

Plates And Glasses

Did you know?
Ego lies in plates and glasses smaller.
I've never seen women
Serve the supposedly superior beings,
Bread and water
In plates and glasses smaller.

Although they consider themselves superior,
They cannot help themselves to what's already on the tables,
With ladles or pour themselves water.

Although they consider themselves superior,
The duties bearing home, kitchen and children Intertwines with a word as small as pride.

Although they consider themselves superior,
They have delicate egos,
Provoked by smaller plates and glasses.

And although they consider themselves superior,
They become inferior
Through their disdaining emotions and decrepit egos.

The Affliction Man Gives

Few voices get lost in the midst of misery.
They pray, beg and seek freedom
At the places they call home.
They listen, obey
And heed to the rules
Made by the people they call love.

Like birds in cages
And plants in pots;
Limiting their dreams and desires
They fear and forgive
"The affliction man gives".

Unclean

Unclean are the women,
Who bleed intermittently
Yet, clean are the women,
Who bleed after their wedding vows.

Brand Me with Your Version of Womanhood

Remember the girl you were in high school

Before you stripped yourself off your girlhood

With hot wax and razors?

Remember the time you were ashamed of your mustache?

The hair on your hands and the colour of your tone?

The man I love often calls me beautiful,

But I doubt truths and untruths!

And I try convincing myself,

They should love me for who I am!

But the advertisements on television tell me otherwise.

Wax your hands babe, veet it;

Complexion matters,

So Fair and Lovely is the key;

Slim is beautiful,

Drink the green tea.

They do not know
That the purpose of hot wax and razors
Is not only to pull out the robust hair;
But to brand me with their own version of womanhood.
To tell me I'm clean without it
And hygienic to the peak.

You call me beautiful love,
But I dare you to call me beautiful
When my hair grows back.

Tinted Windows

I've lived through a generation
That had to cancel tinted windows on cars
Instead of teaching their men they shouldn't abuse.

Roots

Strength grows like brittle roots
And leaves attend a thousand funerals
While burying their older selves.
They grow anew
With blooming buds stronger roots.

If Men Wrote Sensuality Sensibly

If men wrote sensuality sensibly
My skin would have red marks
From bras and bra straps;
I wouldn't have multiple orgasms everyday
Nor would I be capable of holding in my period
Like it's nature's call.
My face would have blemishes
And my legs would be hairy;
The 'o' of my mouth and the creases of my eyebrows
Would look awful in the act of love making;
The breadbasket of my tummy,
Would convex without conviction
And my thighs would bear razor bumps.
I often wish I'd look
Like the flawless fictional women that men write of
With less flesh on their bones

And purity in their tones.
Hair as smooth as feathers
And breasts arched perfectly.
But I'm real
With glitches on my body
And maybe that is how it's supposed to be.

Radhe's Raas

I await this night
In my anklets and bangles.
Like Radha awaits Krishna's presence
For the raas each night.
Like Radha awaits Krishna's presence
For tenderness each night.
The fragrance of Champa in my braids;
The sweet chimes of ornaments in my neck;
The red vermilion on my forehead;
And the seven yards, blue and yellow await
Your ethereal petal like eyes.
In wanting,
Love and faith
As pure as the Ganga
I await this night.

Dear Maa

Dear Maa,
You gave me wings to fly
Ripples of hope
And courage to touch the sky.
But tell me
Why my wings are seized at 21?
Or cut into two
With toxic knives.

Tell me,
Why can't I love my dreams?
Or the poetry that runs through my veins?

Tell me,
Why can't I love men?
Apart from the one's you non consensually arrange?

Tell me,

Why I'm burdened
With responsibilities bitter and new
The same that does not apply
To the gender different from you?

Tell me Maa,
Why have my wings been cut off?
And my dreams shattered.
Into a million pieces that are hard to put back.

Chasing Rainbows

Female friendships and sleepovers
Are like birds that have escaped cages,
Flying high amidst the skies in gladness.
We're laying lazily on a mattress,
Drinking rum out of tetra packs and
Whiskey out of tea cups
Sharing cigarettes whilst losing count.
It's like confetti falling in a dull lit room,
Except the confetti are your female friends
Full of vivid and colourful conversations.

It's divine in its own way
And the happiness so swell.
Many loves come and go
But the flock sticks together;
Like the waves in the sea
And every colour under the sun
Female friendships are sublime.

Women And Climaxes

In the dark hours of my being
I make love to myself.
It's a late hour, maybe two;
And in all the silence and sublimity,
I want a calamity, cascading.
And with every string I touch,
I'm a mythical bird, singing.
And while I close my eyes and bite my lips;
I feel a euphoria erupting.
Like bright stars, diamonds and blissful blithe-ness.
It feels enticing to be a woman and
To touch and feel and know it's real.
There lies no pain or conceal
Or shame or struggle,
But ceaseless blithely brimming climaxes.

Women of the Home

Woman of the home
"Are inept, unproductive and uneducated" you say.
Woman of the home
"Watch Soaps, gossip and sleep all day" you say
Woman of the home
"Are talent-less, uninteresting and unaware" you say.
But without "Woman of the home"
You cannot find your socks or your ties.

You may notice,
That food doesn't appear magically on tables
Nooks and corners are clean and tidy
And that flower vase is in its place.

You cannot make the bed,
Nor can you put the towel out for drying.
You cannot find pressed shirts,
Nor will you find your things in place

And when you come back home,
Do you not wonder how everything is in place again?

Because women of the home
Are brimming with love and patience.
Because women of the home
Make your house a home.

To My Love

To my love,
I wanted to say "no"
But my consent to say "no"
Was snatched away from me.

Bloom

When my hope had been buried deep,
I'd water it
Hoping a flower would bloom,
But a draught hit my heart
And I was devoid of love and happiness.

One day rain came, in the form of you.
A small leaf had sprung from my heart.

Love had encompassed my heart and rain had planted new hope.
My heart now feels full
And a mighty red hibiscus
Now blooms in love and hope.

I've Learnt Over the Years

A new born suckles for milk and life

While people howl with disgust and obscenities.

I've learnt over years of torment that women's bodies have turned political; Regulated more than our inadequate laws and doused into labels of shame and stigma.

I've learnt over the years that

They make profits off our cleavages

While advertising cars and deodorants

And aftershaves and razors.

Objectified objects

Our breasts are only meant for pleasure, labels and profits;

But for feeding, an abominable sin.

I've learnt over the years that

Low necklines meant we aren't allowed to be victims

Only whores asking for it regardless of the crimes and misuse.

You may call a woman lewd and filthy

But I cannot see why a mother shouldn't feed her child.

Nor can I find meaning in advertisements that objectify.

Our bodies are mere playthings

Meant for lust, but not for life.

They cash in on our cleavages

Build brands over our skins

And subtly teach us, "women are nothing but objects meant for lustful desires and sensual acts.

About the Author

Vaishnavi S Kabadi

Vaishnavi S Kabadi is a poet, working on her debut mythology novel, centered around a female protagonist.

Her work has been published in two anthologies, "Shades of A Woman" and "Fragile Abstractions". She is an artist and poet with a keen interest in social change, aiming to use her voice to shatter existing stereotypes and improve the lives of women in all sections of society.

www.ingramcontent.com/pod-product-compliance
Lightning Source LLC
LaVergne TN
LVHW041635070526
838199LV00052B/3375